How Izzy Bear Found Her Shadow

First Printing, 2013

ISBN 10 0615809391
ISBN 13 9780615809397

Printed in the United States of America

How Izzy Bear Found Her Shadow

Written by Chris Sanders

Illustrated by Rosemarie Gillen

I would like to dedicate this book to my wonderful family. Thanks first to my wife Kim for being my best friend and companion for over twenty years now, today and forever into the future. I could not have asked for a better wife, mother of my children or partner to go through all of life's ups and downs with.

Next, I dedicate this book to my pride and joy of my life- my children, Peyton and Parker. You guys are the inspiration for this book in the fact that I want both of you to realize to always be happy with just who you are and not try to be something you are not. Remember to give your best efforts in everything you do in life and you will succeed at anything you want to do.

Finally, I want to thank my parnets Lester and Carolyn for giving me the life lessons to become the best husband and father that I can be and providing me with a loving home to grow up in and showing me how to do the same for my family.

P.S.Thanks also to my illustrator Rosemarie Gillen. You truly helped me to capture and put into view my vision of who Izzy Bear is. You brought Izzy and her friends to life in this book for all to enjoy and learn from.

One morning Izzy Bear woke up and just as she always does, she walked down the lane to go see her friend Duck.

"Good morning Duck!" she said.

"Good morning Izzy Bear, do you want to walk down to the lake today and see who is there?" said Duck.

"Sure, let's go!" said Izzy Bear.

As they started to walk down the road,
Duck let out a startled, "Quack!"

"What is it Duck?" asked Izzy Bear.

"Izzy Bear, where is your shadow?"

Izzy Bear looked down and noticed her shadow was not there.

"Oh Duck, what am I going to do?"

Izzy Bear was very upset because she had never lost her shadow before.

Duck said she could use his for a while if she wanted. She tried stepping in behind him but with Duck's wings that he uses to fly and his long beak that he has, she could tell that his shadow was not going to fit her.

"Don't worry Izzy Bear, let's get down to the lake and see if the others will help us find it," said Duck.

When they reached the lake, many of their friends were there playing.

"Hey everyone, Izzy Bear has lost her shadow and I tried to share mine but it would not fit. Can any of you share yours for today until she can find hers?" asked Duck.

Rabbit was the first to offer.

"Try my shadow on for size Izzy Bear and if it fits, we can share it today," she said.

Izzy Bear was happy to hear this. She tried to step into Rabbit's shadow but with her long ears and body, Izzy Bear could not fit into her shadow at all.

"You can try on mine Izzy Bear," said Opossum.

She tried to step into Opossum's shadow but with his long tail and short legs, it would not fit on her as well.

Finally, Fox came over and said, "Izzy Bear you can try my shadow on for size if you want."

Izzy Bear tried to fit into Fox's shadow but with his big bushy tail and long legs she could see that this was not a good fit for her either.

Izzy Bear's friends were nice to try and share, but none of their shadows would work for her size and special shape.

Izzy Bear became very sad. She was afraid that if she did not find her shadow before night time, it might be lost forever.

Turtle saw what was happening and swam over to see if he could help.

"Hey guy's, what's going on?" he asked.

"Izzy Bear has lost her shadow. We have tried all of our shadows to see if she could share today but none would fit," said Fox.

"Yes, and it will be night soon and time is runing out to find it," said Opossum.

"Where did you last see it Izzy Bear?" asked Turtle.

"The last time I saw it was yesterday in front of my house. I rushed off this morning and before I realized it, it was gone," Izzy Bear exclaimed.

Turtle stood quiet for a moment thinking to himself and then said, "Then it seems the best place to look would be back at your house."

So Izzy Bear and Duck wished their friends good night and headed back to Izzy Bear's home.

As they walked up the stone path to her front door, Duck began to quack loudly and flap his wings wildly.

"Quack, quack, quack! Izzy Bear look, its your shadow!" Duck shouted.

To Izzy Bear's delight she also saw her shadow by the front door. It had been waiting for her right there the whole day.

Izzy Bear ran over to her shadow and stepped on the edge so that they were together again. Izzy Bear was so happy! She saw right away that her shadow was a perfect fit for her.

Then Izzy Bear and Duck danced around happily with their shadows.

With all the noise Momma Bear came out and asked, "What is all this dancing about children?"

"Oh Momma Bear, I had lost my shadow all day and no matter how many other friend's shadows I tried to share, none of them were the right fit for me," said Izzy Bear.

"Izzy Bear, don't you know that we all have our own unique shadow in life? I hope you learned none of us should try to be something other than who we are," said Momma Bear.

"Yes Momma Bear, I realize that now and I am so happy to have my own shadow back!" Izzy Bear said.

At last in her own bed that night, Izzy Bear looked back on the day's events and thought to herself that she and all her friends were unique in their own special way. She realized that she and her friends all cast their own shadow every day in life and to try to fit into being something we are not does not work for any of us.

Looking at her shadow against the moonlit wall in her room, Izzy Bear was very happy. She looked forward to many more adventures that she and her shadow would have together beginning bright and early tomorrow morning.